THIS BOOK BELONGS TO

Barnaby Martin

Richard Scarry's
STORY BOOK

DEAN

This edition first published in 1993 by
Dean, an imprint of Reed Children's Books,
Michelin House, 81 Fulham Road, London SW3 6RB
and Auckland, Melbourne, Singapore and Toronto
by arrangement with Western Publishing Company, Inc.

ISBN 0 603 55243 9

A CIP catalogue record for this book is available at the
British Library.

Printed in China

The stories in this book have also appeared in *Richard Scarry's
Best Bedtime Book Ever, Richard Scarry's Best Storybook
Ever* and *Richard Scarry's Busy, Busy World.*

CONTENTS

Manuel of Mexico

Manuel's wife broke her cooking pot. She needed a new pot to cook her beans in for supper.

"Manuel," she said. "Take this money and go to the market place. Buy a new cooking pot so that you may have hot beans for supper."

Manuel was so excited to be going to the market place. He didn't look where he was going. He kicked a cooking pot by accident and broke it. He paid the man for breaking it.

Pig Lady was cooking beans in her cooking pot. He stepped into the stew by mistake. He said he was sorry.

The smell of Pig Lady's beans made him hungry. He went to Armadillo's restaurant and had a bowl of beans.

When he had finished, he accidentally knocked over the bean pot and spilled the beans.

"I think it is time to go home," he said to himself. "I think I am forgetting something but I can't remember what."

He didn't look where he was going and bumped into Dog.

A pot landed on his head. "Ah, yes, I remember now. I was to buy a cooking pot," Manuel said to himself.

But alas! The pot was stuck on his head.

He went home to his wife.

"I remembered to bring home a cooking pot," he said.

His wife had to break the pot to get it off his head.

Manuel had cold beans for supper.

Sergeant Yukon of the Canadian "Mounties"

It was a peaceful day in Goldtown away up the Canadian Northwest. The door to Sergeant Yukon's police station suddenly flew open.

"Klondike Kid and Tundra Pete are back in town!" said Grubstake Moose.

That meant trouble, for they were the two nastiest men in all Canada.

Sergeant Yukon ran to the door and looked out.

Everyone was running down the street as fast as they could go. Everyone was afraid of those two bullies.

But Sergeant Yukon wasn't afraid.
"I shall take care of them," he said to himself as he marched bravely up the street.

Just look at that ugly Klondike Kid. He has taken a lollipop away from a little girl and she is crying.

And just look at that nasty Tundra Pete, splashing that nice old lady's dress.
Oh. Doesn't he think he's funny!

"You are both mean bullies," said Sergeant Yukon. "I am taking you to jail." But look out, Sergeant Yukon! I think they mean to hit you!

Sergeant Yukon ducked just in time.

Sergeant Yukon dragged them off to jail. And they stayed there until they learnt not to be bullies any more.

South American Carnival

Everyone was going to fly to the carnival in the beautiful city of Rio de Janeiro.

A carnival is such fun!

Everyone was going to sing and to dance and to eat. Everyone, that is, but Noah, the Boa Constrictor. He didn't care about singing, and he had no feet to dance with. He was just going to eat.

The plane was full and ready to take off. But, just at the last minute, Aunty Ant came running.

"There is always room for one more," said the stewardess.

Oh me! Oh my! She was wrong!
That little Aunty Ant was just
one too many! The plane split open!
   "How will we ever get to the
carnival now?" they all asked.
   "I think I know how," said Noah.
"Just everyone stay where they are."

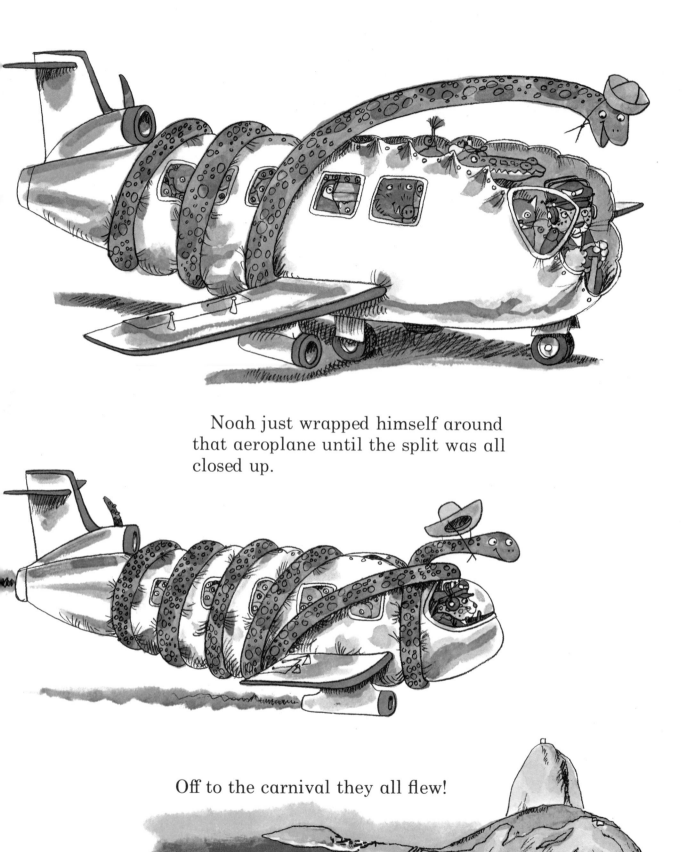

Noah just wrapped himself around that aeroplane until the split was all closed up.

Off to the carnival they all flew!

Everyone had a splendid time.
Everyone sang, and danced, and ate.
Everyone, that is, except Noah.
Noah just ate.

15

Ernst, the Swiss Mountain Climber

Ernst Goat could climb up mountains. He could climb down mountains, too.

Heidi Goat had a cow who could climb up mountains. But her cow couldn't climb down.

One day when Ernst was playing his long alphorn Heidi came running and said, "My cow has climbed the mountain again!"

Ernst climbed up the mountain. "This is the last time I will bring Heidi's cow down," he said.

He tied a rope around the cow and started to lower her. Suddenly he slipped!...

...and fell!!!!

Ernst caught a branch with his axe just in time.

"I will never again climb that mountain to bring your cow down," he said.

The very next day, Heidi came to Ernst and said, "My cow has climbed the mountain again!"

Ernst grabbed his rope and axe.
"This is the last time I will bring your cow down from the mountain," he said.

I wonder if it was?

17

Pierre,
the Paris Policeman

Pierre was directing traffic when
suddenly he heard someone shout,
"Stop that robber! Stop that robber!"
  A robber had stolen some jewels from
a shop. The robber ran to his car.

Pierre hopped on his bicycle and chased
after the robber. He blew his whistle
furiously. Brrrrrreeeeeeeeeet!

Through the crowded streets they raced.

Suddenly the robber's car crashed into a pavement cafe. The robber ran into the restaurant.

Brrrrrrrrrreeeeeeeeeeet!

Pierre followed him.
Brrrrrrrrreeeeeeeeeet! . . . .

. . . . into the kitchen.
"Where is the robber?"
he roared at the chef.
The chef hadn't seen any robber.

Poor Pierre! He had
lost the robber.
"Mmmmmmm, that soup
you are cooking smells
good," said Pierre.
"May I taste it?"

He put in his paw.
Look at what he found!
The robber! The robber
had hidden in the soup.

Before Pierre took
the robber away to
be punished, they all
had some soup.

"This is the best
soup ever!" said the
chef to the robber.
"Perhaps after you
have been punished
for stealing, you will
come back and help
me make soup all the
time? We will call it
'Robber Soup'."
Everyone thought
that that was a good
idea.

Just an Ordinary Day with Babykins

When the alarm clock goes off in the morning, Father Cat jumps out of bed.

Babykins is already awake.

Here he is, all washed and ready for breakfast. My, what a fine fellow!

Babykins likes to have breakfast with Father. Father likes to have breakfast with his newspaper. Oops! Be careful, Father! You're spilling the milk!

Mother Cat can pour four cups of coffee at once, three for Father and one for herself.

Oh, oh, Father. There's no time to drink your last cup of coffee. You are going to be late for your train.

Father Cat finishes his breakfast while running to catch his train.

Hurry, Father. Faster, faster. He runs, he leaps...

Thump! He misses his train!

Luckily a bus comes along. Father manages to catch it.

But he can't find his ticket. Where do you suppose he put it? Poor Father. Will he ever get to work?

Meanwhile, at home, Mother Cat
is trying to get Babykins dressed.
But that little rascal wants to
play with his hammer.

"Babykins!" says Mother. "Please
sit still while I tuck in your shirt."

Now Babykins is dressed in his nice
clean clothes. He is trying to copy
the television commercial. Quick,
Kitty, turn around!

Today the Cats are having stew
for lunch. Babykins loves stew.
He loves to wear it on his head.

I think that this must be the only
neat way to feed Babykins. Good
for you, Kitty!

It is bathtime! That's why Mother has her raincoat on. She is going to give Babykins his bath. Look out, Babykins! Mother is after you.

Now Babykins is all nice and clean. Look out, Mother! You should have kept your raincoat on.

At last Babykins is ready for his nap. Sleep well, Babykins. You're such a good little boy when you're asleep.

Be quiet, Tom! Babykins is trying to sleep. RRRRRRRR!! Tom is cleaning the rug with the vacuum cleaner.

Grandma doesn't want Tom and Kitty to wake Babykins, so she has taken them to the toy shop. She is going to buy them each a present for helping her around the house.

Oh, what a beautiful tuba Tom has found!

Grandma is getting her money to pay for the tuba. Tom, come out of there this instant!

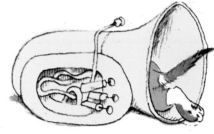

Kitty has found the present she wants, too.
"Oh, Kitty," says Grandma. "Did you have to pick the biggest doll in the shop?"

Poor Grandma had to carry those big presents all the way home. She is all worn out.

She's sleeping now, but Babykins is awake!
No, Babykins, no...

BLAAAAT! Oh, Babykins, I didn't know you could play the tuba.

29

Why, look at that.
Babykins can play the
piano, too. He is
such a talented fellow!

Tom is playing with Babykins
to keep him out of trouble.
What fine musicians!

"All right, boys," says Mother.
"*That* is enough music for one day.
Why don't you do something
quiet?"
So Tom and Babykins decide to
build with their blocks. What a
wonderful tower they have made.
What will they think of next?

They've thought of
building a wall! Now they
will have to think of a
way for Father to get in
the door.
CRASH! They thought
of a way.

After a hard day's work, Father relaxes with his paper. Babykins relaxes with Father's watch.

Babykins is a curious little fellow. He likes to find out how things work.

No, Babykins, a watch does not work like that. Oh, that rascal Babykins. He has broken Father's watch!

After supper, Father settles down with his paper again. Mother turns on the light. Tom and Kitty are doing their homework. But where is Babykins?

Here he is, the little rascal. He wants to play with Father.

Poor Father is too tired. He wants to take a nap. I think you should stop that right now, Babykins!

At last Father is awake. Now he's trying to watch television. Babykins is still climbing about.

It is just before bedtime. Father always reads a good-night story to Babykins. Babykins just loves a good story.

And so off to bed goes Babykins. Goodnight, Babykins. Sleep tight.

Aaah. At last Babykins is in bed. Now everyone can relax. But wait a minute. What's that noise I hear? Oh, no ... Babykins wants a glass of water!

Here is Babykins sound asleep at last. Sweet little Babykins. He's such a good little baby. Sleep tight, Babykins.

Babykins' Birthday

Babykins is writing the invitations to his birthday party.

Guess how old he will be?

Babykins is all dressed up for the party. He is wearing his new clothes ... and chocolate and vanilla ice cream.

The party has begun. I think Squeaky's balloon is a little too big for him.

Tom plays "Happy Birthday to Babykins" on his funny horn.

As Tom calls everyone to the table, a neighbour rings the doorbell to complain about all the noise

Kitty wants her dolls to have some birthday cake, too. "Here, you carry this one," she says to Flossie.

Hooray! The cake is being served. Kitty and Tom are ready for a piece, but where is Babykins?

Here he is, the funny fellow. He is entertaining his guests with some tricks.

Here he is pretending to be a knight fighting a fierce dragon. Very good, Babykins!

Here is Babykins balancing a dish. What skill! What daring!

What happened?

Nurse Matilda of Australia

Nurse Matilda was very busy in the hospital. She gave Anteater his medicine for his sore throat.

She put an icebag on Cassowary's head and took his temperature.

She bandaged Bandicoot's ear and gave him a book to read.

She gave Goat a glass of orange juice and a straw to drink it with.

She put naughty Bunny Rabbit back into bed for the nineteenth time. Isn't he awful! He got out again as soon as she left.

I wonder where Nurse Matilda was going to now?

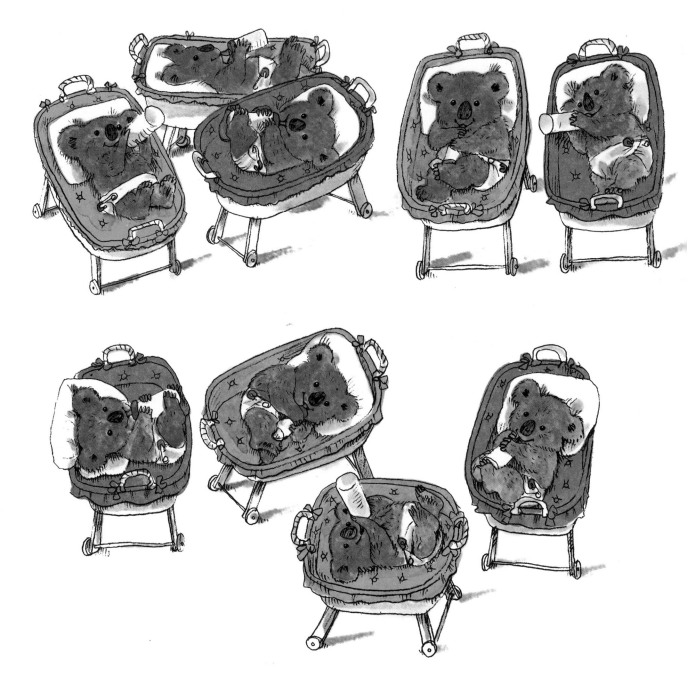

Why, she was going to the nursery
to give the Koala babies their bottles.
Now all the Koala babies are happy with
their bottles. But Nurse Matilda has
one bottle left. Whom can that be for,
I wonder?

Why, of course! It is for her own
little baby, Billybong.
Drink it all up, Billybong!

Albert,
The Belgian Barge Captain

Albert's barge was sailing merrily along the canal. Albert's wife was putting the washing on the line.

Pieter Pig was dreaming of catching a big fish.

"A fish! A fish!
I caught a fish!" said the pig.

"You caught a barge captain!" said Albert, "Now how will I ever get back on my barge?"

"There is only one way," said Pieter Pig.

"This is the way...

...to do it!"

Albert's trousers tore.

And Albert landed, upside down, in his pyjama trousers!

"Why are you wearing your pyjamas in the middle of the day?" his wife asked him. "And how *ever* did you tear your nice new trousers?"

Smokey, the New York Fireman

Smokey was taking a nap in his fire station.

Look! There is smoke coming from Kathleen Kitty's window!

The fire alarm rang!
BRRRRRRRRRRRRINNNNNNGGGGGG!!

He slid down a pole into his fire engine below.

Smokey put on his hat, his boots and his raincoat.

Clang! Clang! Get out of the way!
Officer Murphy stopped the cars.

A pie van didn't get out of the
way in time.
The sky was full of blueberry
pies ... and the pieman!

41

Kathleen Kitty was screaming to be saved.

Smokey climbed up the
ladder and saved her.

He turned his
hose on the fire.
SWOOOOOOOOSH!
and the fire was out.

He turned his hose on his fire
engine. SWOOOOOOOOSH!
and his fire engine
was red again.

He turned his hose on the
pieman. SWOOOOOOOOOOSH!
and the pieman was clean again.

Then they all went inside to see
what the fire was all about. It was
a blueberry pie which had burnt
in the oven.

So Kathleen Kitty
        made another . . .

. . . and they all sat down and ate it.

Angus, the Scottish Bagpiper

When Officer Angus said "Stop!" people heard him and they stopped!

He told the cars to *STOP* so that the Macintosh family could cross the street. The cars stopped.

He told two silly boys to *stop fighting*. The silly boys stopped.

He told Sandy to please *STOP DANCING* on the grass. Sandy stopped.

He had spent a busy day telling people to stop doing something. Now he was going to go home and have fun playing his bagpipes.

Angus marched about his house playing his bagpipes.

"SCREECH SCREECH OOOHAAAH OOOOHAAAAH!"

Oh such a horrible ferocious noise he made!

"NYANNGGGG NYANNGGGG NYANNGGGGGGGGG!"

The sound of his bagpipes could be heard all over town.

"Angus, please STOP!" all the people cried. But Angus was playing so loudly he couldn't hear. And the longer he played the louder he played, and the bigger his bagpipes swelled up.

"ANGUS, PLEASE STOP!!!" the people cried even louder. But Angus couldn't hear them.

Louder and louder he played, and bigger and BIGGER his bagpipes grew.

"ANGUS, PLEASE STOP!!!!" the people roared.

Fortunately for the townspeople, the bagpipes burst, and Angus STOPPED.

Couscous, the Algerian Detective

Couscous was the best detective in Algiers. He was very good at disguising himself to look like someone else.

Couscous is in disguise as he walks past the robbers' den of Pepe le Gangstair. He is trying to think of a way to get inside the robbers' den and capture Pepe and his band of dirty rats.

Can you tell which one is Couscous? No! You can't— because Couscous is so good at disguising himself!

Suddenly Couscous had a good idea. He hurried back to the police station, where his cat and mouse assistants were waiting. He took off his disguise and told them of his plan.

"You have a very clever plan, Couscous!" they all agreed.

That night when it was dark, a small group came to the door of the robbers' den and knocked. Knock! Knock! Knock!

"Who is knocking at my door?" growled Pepe le Gangstair.

"It is I, the pretty dancing girl Fatima, with my troupe of musicians," a soft sweet voice answered. "We have come to entertain you."

"Come in, come in," said Pepe. He opened the door and let them in.

Oh, how beautifully Fatima danced! She was magnificent!

"MORE! MORE!" shouted Pepe.

"I have more for you," said Fatima, "but first I must blindfold you, as I have a big surprise."

So she blindfolded Pepe and the robbers and led them out of the door....

...into the police van! The robbers were prisoners!
  They had been captured by that clever master of disguise
COUSCOUS!!! My! That Couscous is a clever fellow.

Police Officer Louis is everyone's friend. He is very smart. He says:

"Cross the street at the crossing. Always look both ways to see that no cars are coming. Don't run! Always walk!"

Officer Montey of Monaco

"Never throw anything at someone. You might hurt them."

"Never, never play where there is deep water. There might not be anyone around to pull you out!"

"Never push or hit anyone. No one likes a bully."

DANGER

"Never lean out of a car window."

"Never chase a ball into the street."

"Play on the pavement or in your garden. Never play in the street."

"Never go anywhere with someone you don't know."

"Behave yourself and act like a little lady or gentleman when you are in a car."

"And whatever you do, don't bring home stray alligators! They might bite!"

Glip and Glop,
the Greek Painters

Mrs. Metropolus asked Glip and Glop to come and paint her house.

She didn't care what colours they painted it on the inside. But she did insist that the outside of the house be painted blue and white.

She asked Glip and Glop to mind her little boy, Percy, while she went shopping.

"Remember! Paint the outside blue and white," she said as she left.

Glip painted the living room.
It was beautiful.

Glop painted a funny wolf
on Percy's bedroom wall.

They both painted a happy sun on the dining-room ceiling.

And when they had finished painting the inside of the house, they went outside to paint the outside of the house.

"Don't forget ... blue and white," Glip said to Glop.

Glip painted two sides of the house blue and white.

And Glop painted two sides of the house blue and white.

Oh, look what they have done! Half the house has blue sides with white windows, and the other half has white sides with blue windows. Mrs. Metropolus would be furious.

But when Mrs. Metropolus came home, she was very pleased. "Why, it is just like having two houses," she said.

Ukulele Louie,
the Hawaiian Fisherman

Every day, Ukulele Louie threw
his fishing net into the water.

And every day he pulled his net
out of the water. It was always
full of fish.

Then gaily singing and playing
his ukulele, he took his fish and
sold them to his good friend, Joe,
who owned a restaurant.

"I wish I could be a cook in a
restaurant instead of fishing every
day," Louie said to Joe. "I could
make all kinds of good things to
eat. Yum Yum!"

"Very well," said Joe. "Put on
this cook's hat and see what
you can cook up. I have to go
out but I will be back in a few
minutes. Just try to be neat."
Joe left and Louie went into
the kitchen.

He put the fish in the refrigerator. He knocked over the milk while he was taking out some eggs.

He poured a jar of vinegar into a bowl. He put two dozen eggs in the bowl and beat them with a whisk.

He went to the sink to wash the whisk. He forgot to turn the tap off.

He tried to shake some ketchup into the bowl but it wouldn't come out. He shook and shook.
The ketchup came out.

He carried the bowl across the kitchen.
The door opened.
Joe had returned.

"I am afraid you will never be a good cook," said Joe. "You should have used apple sauce instead of ketchup."
"Yes. I think you are right," said Louie.

And so Ukulele Louie went back to fishing, and singing, and playing his ukulele, and he never wanted to cook anything ever again.

Mario, the Venetian Gondolier

Mario had a melon boat. Now, a melon boat is very useful, but it is not beautiful, like a gondola. Mario worked hard selling melons, so that one day he would have enough money to buy a beautiful gondola.

"Just look at that pretty gondola all decorated with flowers," he said to himself. "It must be going to a wedding."

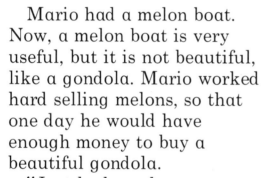

Sure enough! The gondola stopped at a palace. Tina, who was a very beautiful princess, came out with her father. The gondola would take her to church to be married.

Oh! What a shame! Tina is too big for the gondola! How will she ever get to the church to be married?

Have no fear. Here comes Mario! He is strong because he is always lifting melons. He lifts Tina and her father into his boat.

Mario rowed them to the church. Everyone thought it was very funny to see all the melons going to a wedding.

Tina was married to Toni. She was so happy she kissed Toni. Tina's father was so happy he kissed Mario. If it hadn't been for Mario there would have been no wedding.

Tina's father gave Mario a gondola as a present. He is now a real gondolier. He sings happily as he paddles along the canals. But when there is a holiday Mario brings out his melon boat.

For you see . . .

...Tina and Toni now have lots
of children, and they need a strong
and sturdy boat to carry them. Yes!
A very strong and sturdy boat!

Dr. Krunchchew of Russia

On Monday, Dr. Krunchchew examined Lion's teeth.

On Tuesday, he examined Alligator's teeth.

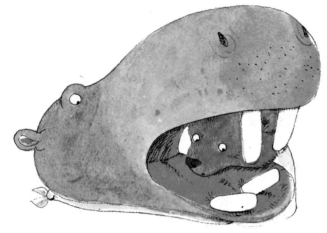

On Wednesday, he looked at Hippopotamus' teeth.

On Thursday, Walrus asked Dr. Krunchchew, "Don't you ever get tired of looking at teeth?"

"Certainly not!" said Dr. Krunchchew. "I LOVE teeth!"

On Friday, he cleaned a nice old Grandmother's teeth. "What have you been eating ?" he asked. Grandma wouldn't say.

"Very fine molars you have, Mr. Mole," laughed Dr. Krunchchew on Saturday.

On Sunday, Mrs. Krunchchew said,
"You have been looking at teeth
all week. You need a rest. Go and
look at something different. Why don't
you go to the Natural History Museum
and look at birds and flowers
and other things?"

So Dr. Krunchchew
went to the museum,
and looked at birds
and flowers ... and ...

WHALE
PLEASE
DO NOT
TOUCH

...and other things.

Hans, the Dutch Plumber

Hans lived in Holland. Somehow or other Hans always managed to come home from work soaking wet. This made his wife very angry.

Sometimes he would get wet because he forgot his umbrella.

Sometimes he would get wet mending a leaky pipe.

But he really got wet when he didn't look where he was going and fell into a canal.

Now much of the land of Holland is below the level of the sea. The people built dikes to keep the sea water out. If a dike was to get a hole in it, the water would pour through the hole and all the land would be covered with water and fish.

One day Hans saw a big leak in the dike. There was water pouring through it. A tourist was waiting to take a picture of someone putting something in the hole to stop the leak in the dike.

Hans put the tourist in the hole to stop the leak in the dike. Now a tourist is not the best thing for mending leaks so Hans rode off to get some bags of sand. When he returned he took the tourist out of the hole and filled the hole with bags of sand.

The burgomaster gave Hans a medal. His wife would be very pleased. He had mended the biggest leak ever and he hadn't got the littlest bit wet.

On his way home it started to rain. He had remembered to bring his umbrella. He would arrive home nice and dry. Today his wife wouldn't be angry with him.

But wait! Hans doesn't see that the bridge is open!

His wife is very angry.

Professor Dig and his Egyptian Mummy

Professor Dig had been out in the desert all day digging.

He dug and dug, until finally he dug up a beautiful mummy!

He would take it to the Cairo museum where everyone could go and look at it and say "OOH! AAH!! It was *so* beautiful!

The Professor was very hot and thirsty when he arrived in Cairo. He decided to stop at Ali Baba's restaurant.

"Will you watch my mummy for a few minutes while I sit and drink a cold glass of lemonade?" the Professor asked Ali Baba.

Now, Ali Baba couldn't see very well. He thought that the professor's MUMMY was the Professor's real live MOTHER!!

"What kind of a son is that who will leave his mother standing after a hot trip while he sits down and has a cold lemonade?" Said Ali to the mummy, "You must be very tired. Permit me to sit you in a chair."

"Oh you poor woman," said Ali. "You are so stiff from your long journey, you can't even bend to sit down. Perhaps if you were to lie down with your feet in the air, you would feel better."

"Ah, yes, I can see you are looking better already," he said. "Your dress is a little dusty, though. Let me dust you off."

"Ah, the music is playing in the Palm Room. Dum de dum de dum. May I have this dance while we are waiting for your son? Dum de dum. Ah, madam you are a delightful dancer."

Just then the Professor came along. He thanked Ali for taking care of his mummy and carried it away.

"Oh, how that boy treats his poor old mother," said Ali. "IMAGINE!! Carrying her on his head! I wouldn't treat my mummy that way! Would YOU?"

Sneef, the Best Detective in Europe

Sneef was the best detective in all Europe. He was always ready to help Police Chiefs at any time and in any place.

One rainy day in Paris, Sneef received a phone call from the Chief of Police of Nice. He wanted Sneef to come right away.

Oh! How sad. Tomorrow would be Sneef's birthday and he had hoped to spend it at home eating ice cream and cake.

"I wonder who all those bad-looking men are," said Sneef to himself as the train conductor showed him to his bedroom.

"They seem to be watching me!" Sneef was a little frightened.

At every station they stopped at that night, Sneef could see more evil-looking men getting on the train.

And they all carried violin cases! What mischief were they up to?

Sneef was very frightened! He shivered and hid under the bed.

The train arrived in Nice in the morning. Sneef crawled out from under the bed and saw those mysterious men looking at him.

Before he got off the train he put on sunglasses to protect his eyes from the bright sunlight.

As he stepped off the train, he saw all the Police Chiefs of Europe!

They had thrown away their disguises and were playing "Happy Birthday to You, Dear Sneefy!" on their violins.

It was a surprise birthday party!

They all went to the beach and ate ice cream and cake until they could eat no more. It was Sneef's best birthday party ever!

Two Norwegian Fishermen

Uncle Olaf and Uncle Oscar had nine nieces and nephews waiting for them on the dock. They were waiting for Uncle Olaf and Uncle Oscar to catch a big fish for supper.

Uncle Olaf caught a tin can. Uncle Oscar didn't catch anything.

Uncle Olaf caught a rubber boot. Uncle Oscar didn't catch anything.

Uncle Olaf caught an old tyre. Uncle Oscar didn't catch anything.
What kind of a fisherman is Uncle Oscar anyway? He can't catch anything.

WOW!! Uncle Oscar caught a fish.

He paddled back to the dock where the nine nieces and nephews were waiting . . .

. . . and that night, they had the best fish supper ever!

Sven Svenson's Busy Day

Sven Svenson lived with Mrs. Sven Svenson on a farm in Sweden. He ate a gherkin for breakfast.

He put on his straw hat and he went to the barn to milk his cow. His cow kicked over the milk pail.

He fed his hens and gathered their eggs.

He went to the railway station to pick up a package which was coming on the train from the city.

It was a present for his wife. He tried it on for fun.

When he got home, he gave the hat to his wife. She gave him a gherkin for lunch.

After lunch Sven brought the hay in from the fields. His cow loves to eat hay and straw.

He put the hay into the barn. The wind blew his straw hat up into the barn. He would climb up and get it after he had a drink of water. It was a hot day and he was dry and thirsty.

He went to the well for a drink. He fell in!

Mrs. Svenson came and pulled him out. Her new hat fell in the well.

It was the end of a busy day. Sven Svenson and Mrs. Sven Svenson ate seven gherkins for supper.

Sven Svenson's cow found Sven Svenson's hat in Sven Svenson's barn. Sven Svenson's cow ate Sven Svenson's hat for supper.

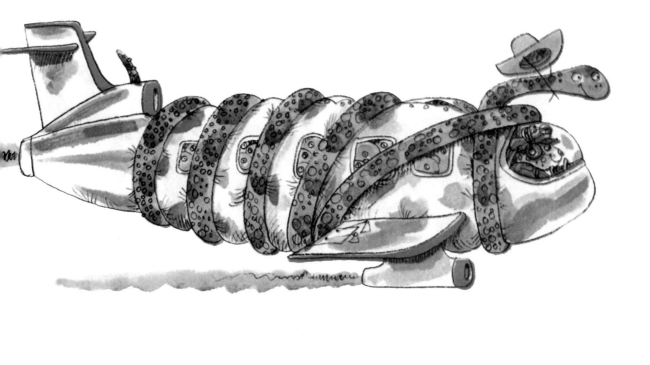

Pip Pip
Goes to London

Pip Pip Cat went to London
to seek his fame and fortune
in the service of the Queen.

First, he went to the Tower of London, to see if he could be a Beefeater, which means a Guardian of the Queen's jewels. No! They didn't need any more guards.

When he went to the Queen's palace, the guard wouldn't talk to him. He was too busy guarding the Queen.

In Whitehall, where the Household Cavalry are on guard, he was afraid of being stepped upon and so he quickly left.

Pip Pip was very sad. He wouldn't be able to serve the Queen after all.

"The Queen must be very sad too," he said to himself. "She has lost her ring."

He passed a fountain into which people had thrown pennies for good luck. He saw something which didn't look like a penny! It was golden! It glittered!

It was a ring!
Maybe it was the Queen's ring!!
He showed it to a policeman.

They hurried off to see the Queen. It was the Queen's ring! She was very happy to have it back.

The Queen made Pip Pip "The Queen's Guard of Her Majesty's Fountains".

Every day, he scooped out the "good luck" pennies.

The Queen used the money to buy food for the poor stray cats who had no homes and lived in alleys.

Wasn't she a nice Queen?